I Love My Pet
SPIDER

Alexis Roumanis

LET'S READ
AV²
BY WEIGL™
ADDED VALUE • AUDIO VISUAL

www.av2books.com

LET'S READ

AV²
BY WEIGL™
ADDED VALUE • AUDIO VISUAL

Go to **www.av2books.com**, and enter this book's unique code.

BOOK CODE

V780447

AV² by Weigl brings you media enhanced books that support active learning.

AV² provides enriched content that supplements and complements this book. Weigl's AV² books strive to create inspired learning and engage young minds in a total learning experience.

Your AV² Media Enhanced books come alive with...

Audio
Listen to sections of the book read aloud.

Video
Watch informative video clips.

Embedded Weblinks
Gain additional information for research.

Try This!
Complete activities and hands-on experiments.

Key Words
Study vocabulary, and complete a matching word activity.

Quizzes
Test your knowledge.

Slide Show
View images and captions, and prepare a presentation.

... and much, much more!

Published by AV² by Weigl
350 5th Avenue, 59th Floor   New York, NY   10118
Websites: www.av2books.com   www.weigl.com

Library of Congress Control Number: 2014934858
ISBN 978-1-4896-1302-8 (hardcover)
ISBN 978-1-4896-1303-5 (softcover)
ISBN 978-1-4896-1304-2 (single-user eBook)
ISBN 978-1-4896-1305-9 (multi-user eBook)

Printed in the United States of America in North Mankato, Minnesota
1 2 3 4 5 6 7 8 9 0   18 17 16 15 14

042014
WEP150314

Senior Editor: Aaron Carr   Art Director: Terry Paulhus

Weigl acknowledges Getty Images as the primary image supplier for this title.

I Love My Pet
SPIDER

CONTENTS

I love my pet spider.
I take good care of her.

4

My pet spider hatched
from an egg.
She could walk around
right after hatching.

My pet spider was two weeks old when I took her home.
She grows the most when she is warm and well fed.

Spiders shed their skin when they grow.

My pet spider has six eyes.
Her large eyes can see sizes,
shapes, and colors.
Her small eyes can see movement.

My pet spider has eight legs. She has four legs on each side of her body.

Claws at the end of each leg are used to hold onto food.

13

14

My pet spider can spin a web.
She uses her web to catch food.

My pet spider eats insects. She likes to eat flies.

Spiders use their fangs to eat.

My pet spider needs to be cared for.
Her web needs to be sprayed
with water every week.

19

20

I make sure my pet spider is healthy.
I love my pet spider.

SPIDER FACTS

These pages provide more detail about the interesting facts found in the book. They are intended to be used by adults as a learning support to help young readers round out their knowledge of each animal featured in the *I Love My Pet* series.

Pages 4–5

I love my pet spider. I take good care of her. There are about 40,000 kinds of spiders. Tarantulas are the most popular kind of spider to keep as pets. Other popular kinds of spiders are wolf spiders, jumping spiders, fishing spiders, and grass spiders. To stay healthy, spiders need a clean cage, food, water, and exercise. Each spider is different, so owners need to learn their spider's likes and dislikes.

Pages 6–7

My pet spider hatched from an egg. She could walk around right after hatching. Spiders are arachnids, not insects. Other types of arachnids include mites, ticks, and scorpions. Spiders lay eggs to have babies. Some kinds of spiders can lay up to 3,000 eggs at one time, while others lay as few as 10 eggs. Most spiders have to fend for themselves when they hatch.

Pages 8–9

My pet spider was two weeks old when I brought her home. She grows fastest when she is warm and well fed. Spiders have hard outer shells called exoskeletons. When a spider grows, it sheds its exoskeleton. This happens most often when a spider is young. The spider grows quickly before a new exoskeleton hardens. Spiders can grow up to 12 inches (30.5 centimeters) long.

Pages 10–11

My pet spider has six eyes. Her large eyes can see sizes, shapes, and colors. Her small eyes can see movement. Spiders may have as many as eight eyes. The number and positioning of the eyes varies from species to species. Spiders have good eyesight from their large, forward-facing eyes. However, the smaller eyes, which are often on the side of a spider's head, can see shadows and the difference between light and dark.

My pet spider has eight legs. She has four legs on each side of her body. Each spider leg has six knees. An eight legged spider has a total of 48 knees. Spider legs are covered in small hairs. These hairs help the spider to feel vibrations. Some spiders have three claws at the end of each leg. Spiders use their middle claw, and the hairs on their legs, to cling to their web.

My pet spider can spin a web. She uses her web to catch food. Spider webs are made from spider silk. This is made in a spider's belly. Web building spiders create a round or square connection between plants, trees, and rocks. Inside this connection, a spider will build a spiral of sticky threads. Small insects get caught in these sticky threads, trapping a spider's food.

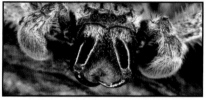

My pet spider eats bugs. She likes to eat flies. Spiders use their fangs to eat. All spiders are carnivorous, or meat eaters. Flies, mosquitoes, and crickets are some of the spider's favorite foods. Some spiders will even eat small fish and mice. Bugs can be collected from the outdoors and placed in the spider's cage once or twice a week. Crickets can be purchased from a local pet store.

My pet spider needs to be cared for. Her web needs to be sprayed with water every week. Spiders should be kept in plastic terrariums. To prevent escape, ensure the air holes in the top of the enclosure are smaller than the spider. A plastic bottle cap can be used as a water dish. The spider's web should be lightly sprayed with water once a week. They drink the water droplets that cling to the web.

I make sure my pet spider is healthy. I love my pet spider. Spider enclosures do not need to be cleaned often. However, pet owners should watch closely for signs of mold, fungus, or mites. If the enclosure needs to be cleaned, carefully place the spider in an empty jar until the cleaning is done. Spiders often curl their legs under their bodies when sick. If this happens, see a veterinarian.

KEY WORDS

Research has shown that as much as 65 percent of all written material published in English is made up of 300 words. These 300 words cannot be taught using pictures or learned by sounding them out. They must be recognized by sight. This book contains 53 common sight words to help young readers improve their reading fluency and comprehension. This book also teaches young readers several important content words, such as proper nouns. These words are paired with pictures to aid in learning and improve understanding.

Page	Sight Words First Appearance
4	good, her, I, my, of, take
6	after, an, around, could, from, right, she,
9	and, grows, home, is, most, old, the, their, they, took, two, was, well, when
11	can, eyes, has, large, see, small
12	are, at, each, end, food, four, on, side, used
15	a, to
16	eats, likes
18	be, every, for, needs, water, with
21	make

Page	Content Words First Appearance
4	spider
6	egg
9	skin, weeks
11	colors, movement, shapes, sizes
12	body, claws, legs
15	web
16	fangs, flies, insects

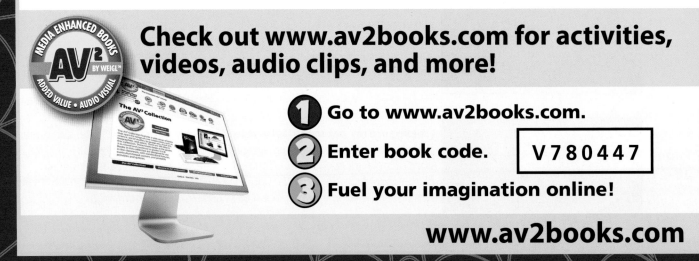

Check out www.av2books.com for activities, videos, audio clips, and more!

1 Go to www.av2books.com.

2 Enter book code. **V 7 8 0 4 4 7**

3 Fuel your imagination online!

www.av2books.com